Kella's Kitten

The Sound of K

by Joanne Meier and Cecilia Minden • illustrated by Bob Ostrom

The Child's World®

Published by The Child's World®
1980 Lookout Drive
Mankato, MN 56003-1705
800-599-READ
www.childsworld.com

The Child's World®: Mary Berendes, Publishing Director
The Design Lab: Design and page production

Library of Congress Cataloging-in-Publication Data
Meier, Joanne D.
  Kella's kitten : the sound of k / by Joanne Meier and
Cecilia Minden ; illustrated by Bob Ostrom.
    p. cm.
  ISBN 978-1-60253-407-0 (library bound : alk. paper)
  1. English language—Consonants—Juvenile literature.
  2. English language—Phonetics—Juvenile literature 3.
Reading—Phonetic method—Juvenile literature. I. Minden,
Cecilia. II. Ostrom, Bob. III. Title.
  PE1159.M458 2010
  [E]—dc22   2010002920

Printed in the United States of America in Mankato, MN.
July 2010
F11538

NOTE TO PARENTS AND EDUCATORS:

The Child's World® has created this series with the goal of exposing children to engaging stories and illustrations that assist in phonics development. The books in the series will help children learn the relationships between the letters of written language and the individual sounds of spoken language. This contact helps children learn to use these relationships to read and write words.

The books in this series follow a similar format. An introductory page, to be read by an adult, introduces the child to the phonics feature, or sound, that will be highlighted in the book. Read this page to the child, stressing the phonic feature. Help the student learn how to form the sound with her mouth. The story and engaging illustrations follow the introduction. At the end of the story, word lists categorize the feature words into their phonic elements.

Each book in this series has been carefully written to meet specific readability requirements. Close attention has been paid to elements such as word count, sentence length, and vocabulary. Readability formulas measure the ease with which the text can be read and understood. Each book in this series has been analyzed using the Spache readability formula.

Reading research suggests that systematic phonics instruction can greatly improve students' word recognition, spelling, and comprehension skills. This series assists in the teaching of phonics by providing students with important opportunities to apply their knowledge of phonics as they read words, sentences, and text.

This is the letter k.

In this book, you will read words that have the **k** sound as in: *kitten, keep, milk,* and *like.*

Kella is a lucky girl.

She has a new kitten.

The kitten's name is Kippy.

The kitten is very soft.

Kella's job is to keep the kitten safe.

Kippy likes to sleep in a basket. It is a warm place.

Kippy likes to drink milk.

Sometimes Kippy drinks

Kella's milk!

Kippy likes to look out the window. He likes to see the birds.

Kella likes to pet Kippy.

Sometimes Kippy scratches.

Ouch!

Kippy sleeps on Kella's bed.

He likes to be warm.

Kella has a new kitten.

Do you have any pets?

Fun Facts

More than 35,000 kittens are born in the United
States every day! Most cats give birth to between
one and eight kittens at a time. One cat in Texas
was the mother of more than 420 kittens over her
lifetime! Mother cats often carry kittens around by the
scruff of their necks. Just like the eyes of a human baby,
a kitten's eyes may change color as it grows older.

Do you like ice cream? Did you know that it takes 10 gallons (38
liters) of milk to make 1 gallon (3.8 L) of ice cream? A dairy cow can
produce up to 90 glasses of milk each day and 200,000 glasses
of milk in its lifetime! But cows aren't our only source of milk—some
farmers also rely on water buffalo, camels, goats, sheep, reindeer,
and horses.

Activity

Learning about a Dairy Farm

Are you curious about how milk gets from a cow to your kitchen
table? If you want to see firsthand, talk to your parents about
contacting a dairy farm in your area. Perhaps you can tour the farm,
or possibly speak to one of the workers there. You can also visit your
local library to check out books that explain this process.

To Learn More

Books
About the Sound of K
Moncure, Jane Belk. *My "k" Sound Box®*. Mankato, MN: The Child's World, 2009.

About Kittens
Berenstain, Stan, Jan Berenstain, and Mike Berenstain. *The Berenstain Bears' New Kitten*. New York: HarperCollins, 2007.

Neye, Emily. *All About Cats and Kittens*. New York: Grosset & Dunlap, 1999.

Royston, Angela. *Kitten*. New York: DK Publishing, 2007

About Milk
Llewellyn, Claire. *Milk*. New York: Children's Press, 1998.

Schaefer, Lola M. *Milk*. Chicago, Heinemann Library, 2008.

Taus-Bolstad, Stacy. *From Grass to Milk*. Minneapolis: Lerner Publications, 2004.

Web Sites
Visit our home page for lots of links about the Sound of K:
childsworld.com/links

Note to Parents, Teachers, and Librarians: We routinely check our Web links to make sure they're safe, active sites—so encourage your readers to check them out!

K Feature Words

Proper Names
Kella
Kippy

Feature Words in Initial Position
keep
kitten

Feature Words in Medial Position
basket
like
lucky

Feature Words in Final Position
drink
look
milk

About the Authors

Joanne Meier, PhD, has worked as an elementary school teacher, university professor, and researcher. She earned her BA in early childhood education from the University of South Carolina, and her MEd and PhD in education from the University of Virginia. She currently works as a literacy consultant for schools and private organizations. Joanne lives in Virginia with her husband Eric, daughters Kella and Erin, two cats, and a gerbil.

Cecilia Minden, PhD, is the former director of the Language and Literacy Program at the Harvard Graduate School of Education. She is now a reading consultant for school and library publications. She earned her PhD in reading education from the University of Virginia. Cecilia and her husband, Dave Cupp, live outside Chapel Hill, North Carolina. They enjoy sharing their love of reading with their grandchildren, Chelsea and Qadir.

About the Illustrator

Bob Ostrom has been illustrating children's books for nearly twenty years. A graduate of the New England School of Art & Design at Suffolk University, Bob has worked for such companies as Disney, Nickelodeon, and Cartoon Network. He lives in North Carolina with his wife Melissa and three children, Will, Charlie, and Mae.